DICK WHITTINGTON
and HIS CAT

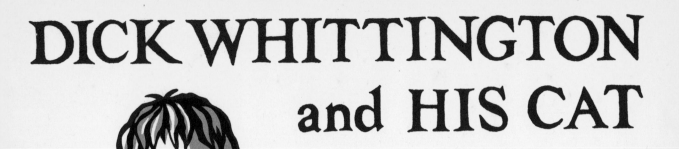

Told and cut
in linoleum by

MARCIA
BROWN

Charles Scribner's Sons
New York   1950

For Alice Dalgliesh
who heard Bow Bells as a child

"Behold a cat whose merit wants a name;
'Twas she that raised poor Whittington to fame."

New Haven Chap Book

DICK WHITTINGTON AND HIS CAT

Long ago in England there lived a little boy named Dick Whittington. Dick's father and mother died when he was very young, and as he was too small to work, he had a hard time of it. The people in the village were poor and could spare him little more than the parings of potatoes and now and then a crust of bread. He ran about the country as ragged as a colt, until one day he met a wagoner on his way to London. "Come along with me," said the wagoner. So off they set together.

Now Dick had heard of the great city of London. It was said that the people who lived there were all fine gentlemen and ladies, that there was singing and music all day long, and that the streets were paved with gold. As for the gold, "I'd be willing to get a bushel of that," said Dick to himself.

But when Dick got to London, how sad he was to find the streets covered with dirt instead of gold! And there he was in a strange place, without food, without friends, and without money. Dick was soon so cold and hungry that he wished he were back sitting by a warm fire in a country kitchen. He sat down in a corner and cried himself to sleep.

A kind gentleman saw him there and said, "Why don't you go to work, my lad?"

"That I would," said Dick, "if I could get anything to do."

"Come along with me," said the gentleman, and he led Dick to a hayfield. There he worked hard and lived merrily until the hay was made.

Now Dick was again forlorn. He wandered back to town, fainting for want of food, and laid himself down at the door of Mr. Fitzwarren, a rich merchant.

Here the cook saw him, and being an ill-natured

hussy, she called out, "On your way there, lazy rogue, or would you like a scalding to make you jump?"

Just then Mr. Fitzwarren came home to dinner. When he saw the dirty, ragged boy lying in his doorway, he said to him, "What ails you, boy? You look old enough to work."

"Sir, I am a poor country lad," said Dick. "I have neither father nor mother nor any friend in the world. I would be glad to work, but I've had no food for three days." Dick then tried to get up, but he was so weak he fell down again.

"Take this lad into the house," Mr. Fitzwarren ordered his servants. "Give him meat and drink. When he is stronger he can help the cook with her dirty work."

Now Dick would have lived happily with this worthy family if he had not been bumped about by the cook.

"Look sharp there, clean the spit, empty the dripping pan, sweep the floor! Step lively or ——!" And down came the ladle on the boy's shoulders. For the cook

was always roasting and basting, and when the spit was still, she basted his head with a broom or anything else she could lay her hands on. When Mr. Fitzwarren's daughter, Alice, saw what was going on, she warned the cook, "Treat that boy more kindly or leave this house!"

Besides the crossness of the cook, Dick had another hardship. His bed was placed in a garret where there were so many rats and mice running over his bed he could never get to sleep.

But one day a gentleman gave Dick a penny for brushing his shoes. The next day Dick saw a girl in the street with a cat under her arm. He ran up to her. "How much do you want for that cat?" he asked.

"Oh, this cat is a good mouser," said the girl. "She will bring a great deal of money."

"But I have only a penny in the world," said Dick, "and I need a cat sadly." So the girl let him have it.

Dick hid his cat in the garret because he was afraid the cook would beat her too. He always saved part of his dinner for her, and Miss Puss wasted no time in killing or frightening away all the rats and mice. Now Dick could sleep as sound as a top.

Not long after this, Mr. Fitzwarren had a ship ready to sail. He called all his servants into the parlor and asked them what they chose to send to trade. All the servants brought something but poor Dick. Since he had neither money nor goods, he couldn't think of sending anything.

"I'll put some money down for him," offered Miss Alice, and she called Dick into the parlor.

But the merchant said, "That will not do. It must be something of his own."

"I have nothing but a cat," said Dick.

"Fetch your cat, boy," said the merchant, "and let her go!"

So Dick brought Puss and handed her over to the captain of the ship with tears in his eyes. "Now the rats and mice will keep me awake all night again," he said. All the company laughed, but Miss Alice pitied Dick and gave him some half-pence to buy another cat.

While Puss was beating the billows at sea, Dick was beaten at home by the cross cook. She used him so cruelly and made such fun of him for sending his cat to sea that the poor boy decided to run away. He packed the few things he had and set out early in the morning on All-Hallows Day. He walked as far as Halloway and sat down on a stone to rest. While he was sitting there wondering which way to go, the Bells of Bow began to ring. Dong! Dong!

They seemed to say to him:
        "Turn again, Whittington,
        Lord Mayor of London."
"Lord Mayor of London!" said Dick to himself. "What wouldn't I give to be Lord Mayor of London and ride in such a fine coach! I'll go back and I'll take the cuffings of the cook, if I'm to be Lord Mayor of London." So home he went. Luckily, he got into the house and about his business before the old cook came downstairs.

Meanwhile the ship with the cat on board was long beating about at sea. The winds finally drove it on the coast of Barbary. Here lived the Moors, a people unknown to the English. They came in great numbers on board to see the sailors and the goods which the captain wanted to trade.

The captain sent some of his choicest goods to the king of the country. The king was so well pleased that he invited the captain and his officer to come to his palace, about a mile from the sea.

Here they were placed on rich carpets, flowered with gold and silver. The king and queen sat at the upper end of the room, and dinner was brought in. No sooner had the servants set down the dishes than an amazing number of rats and mice rushed in. They helped themselves from every dish, scattering pieces of meat and gravy all about.

The captain in surprise turned to the nobles and asked, "Are not these vermin offensive?"

"Oh yes," said they, "very offensive! The King would give half of his treasure to be rid of them. They not

only ruin his dinner, but also attack him in his chamber, even in his bed! He has to be watched while he is sleeping for fear of them!"

The captain jumped for joy. He remembered Whittington and his cat and told the king he had a creature on board the ship that would soon destroy the mice. The king's heart heaved so high at this good news that his turban dropped off his head. "Bring this creature to me!" he cried. "Vermin are dreadful in a court! If she will do what you say, I will load your ship with ivory, gold dust and jewels in exchange for her."

Away flew the captain to the ship, while another dinner was got ready. With Puss under his arm, he returned to the palace just in time to see the rats about to devour the second dinner. At first sight of the rats and mice the cat sprang from the captain's arms. Soon she had laid most of them dead at her feet, while the rest fled to their holes.

The king rejoiced to see his old enemies destroyed.

The queen asked to see Miss Puss. When the captain presented the cat, the queen was a little afraid to touch a creature that had made such havoc among the rats and mice. Finally she stroked her and said, "Puttey, puttey, puttey," for she had not learned English. The captain put the cat on the queen's lap, where she purred and played with her majesty's hand and then sang herself to sleep.

When the king learned that Miss Puss and her kittens would keep the whole country free from rats and mice, he bargained for the whole ship's cargo. He gave ten times as much for Miss Puss as for all the rest.

When the ship was loaded, the captain and his officer took leave of their majesties. A breeze springing up, they hurried on board and set sail for England.

The sun was scarcely up one morning when Mr. Fitz-warren stole from his bed to count over the cash. He had just sat down at his desk in the counting house when somebody came tap, tap-tap at the door.

"Who's there?"

"A friend. I bring you news of the good ship Uni-corn!"

The merchant bustled up in such a hurry that he forgot his gout. He opened the door.

There stood the captain and his officer with a cabinet of jewels and a bill of lading. The merchant lifted up his eyes and thanked Heaven for such a prosperous voyage. They told him about the cat and showed him the caskets of diamonds and rubies they had brought for Dick.

At that the merchant cried out:

"Go call him and tell him of his fame,
And call him Mr. Whittington by name."

Dick was scouring pots in the kitchen and did not want to come into the clean parlor. "The floor is polished, and my shoes are dirty and full of nails." But the merchant made him come in and sit down.

He took Dick by the hand and said, "Mr. Whittington, I sent for you to congratulate you upon your good fortune. The captain has sold your cat to the king of Barbary. She has brought you more riches than I am worth in the world. May you long enjoy them!"

When they showed him the caskets of jewels, Dick laid the whole at his master's feet, but Mr. Fitzwarren

refused it. He offered them to his mistress and his good friend Miss Alice, but they too refused the smallest part. Dick then rewarded the captain and ship's crew for the care they had taken of Puss, and distributed presents to all the servants, even to his old enemy, the cook.

Mr. Fitzwarren advised Mr. Whittington to send for tradesmen to dress him like a gentleman, and offered him his house until he could provide himself with a better. Now when Dick's face was washed, his hair curled, his hat cocked, and he was dressed in a rich suit of clothes, he turned out a genteel young fellow.

In a little time he dropped his sheepish behavior and soon became a sprightly companion. Miss Alice, who formerly looked on him with pity, now saw him in quite another light.

When Mr. Fitzwarren noticed how fond they were of each other, he proposed a match between them. Both parties cheerfully consented.

The Lord Mayor in his coach, Court of Aldermen, Sheriffs, company of stationers, and a number of eminent merchants attended the wedding ceremony. And afterwards all were treated to an elegant entertainment.

Whittington and his bride were called the happiest couple in England. He was chosen Sheriff and was three different times elected Lord Mayor of London. In the last year of his mayoralty Whittington entertained King Henry the Fifth and his Queen.

"Never had Prince such a subject," said Henry, and Whittington replied, "Never had subject such a King!"